"If I had known that this was what it meant to be an apprentice to a Sorcerer, I would never have become one," said Arthur to himself. He was nearly ready to give up his ambition to become a Sorcerer when he thought of a plan.

"If he won't teach me, then I'll find out for myself. I'll watch him secretly while he is working his spells."

Every day, while the Sorcerer was working his magic, Arthur put his ear to the wall and listened to the magic words.

In three years' time he had memorized all the magic words the Sorcerer used.

"Now I'm as good at magic as he is," he boasted to himself, and he could hardly wait for the chance to use the magic words.

One day the Sorcerer said, "Arthur, today I shall be away all day in the town. Fetch in the water, and have my bath ready when I come home at nightfall."

"Now's my chance! I can work my magic, at last!" said Arthur, and he tried out some magic words.

"A bird! A bird! I'm flying in the sky!"

Instantly Arthur changed into a bird, and with a flap of his wings soared up into the sky.

Arthur was so excited he didn't know what to do with himself. He tried another magic word, and now he became a fish. Next he turned into a tiger, and then into a deer.

When he became hungry, he spoke a word and a feast was laid before him.

Suddenly, it began to grow dark.

"Ah! I forgot the bath," he cried.

It was too late to start carrying water from the river to fill the tub.

"I can use my magic for this, too," he decided. So he went down to the river and called out in the Sorcerer's magic language, "Flow, river, flow! Swell, river, swell! Enough to fill the bath."

Before his eyes the river began to flow and swell, until it almost overflowed its banks.

Next, the apprentice got an old broom and, addressing it, said, "Broom, old broom! Stand on your feet! Lift up your head! Draw water, draw! Bring buckets, draw water!"

As he spoke, the old broom sprang up and, carrying a bucket, hopped to the river with lightning speed.

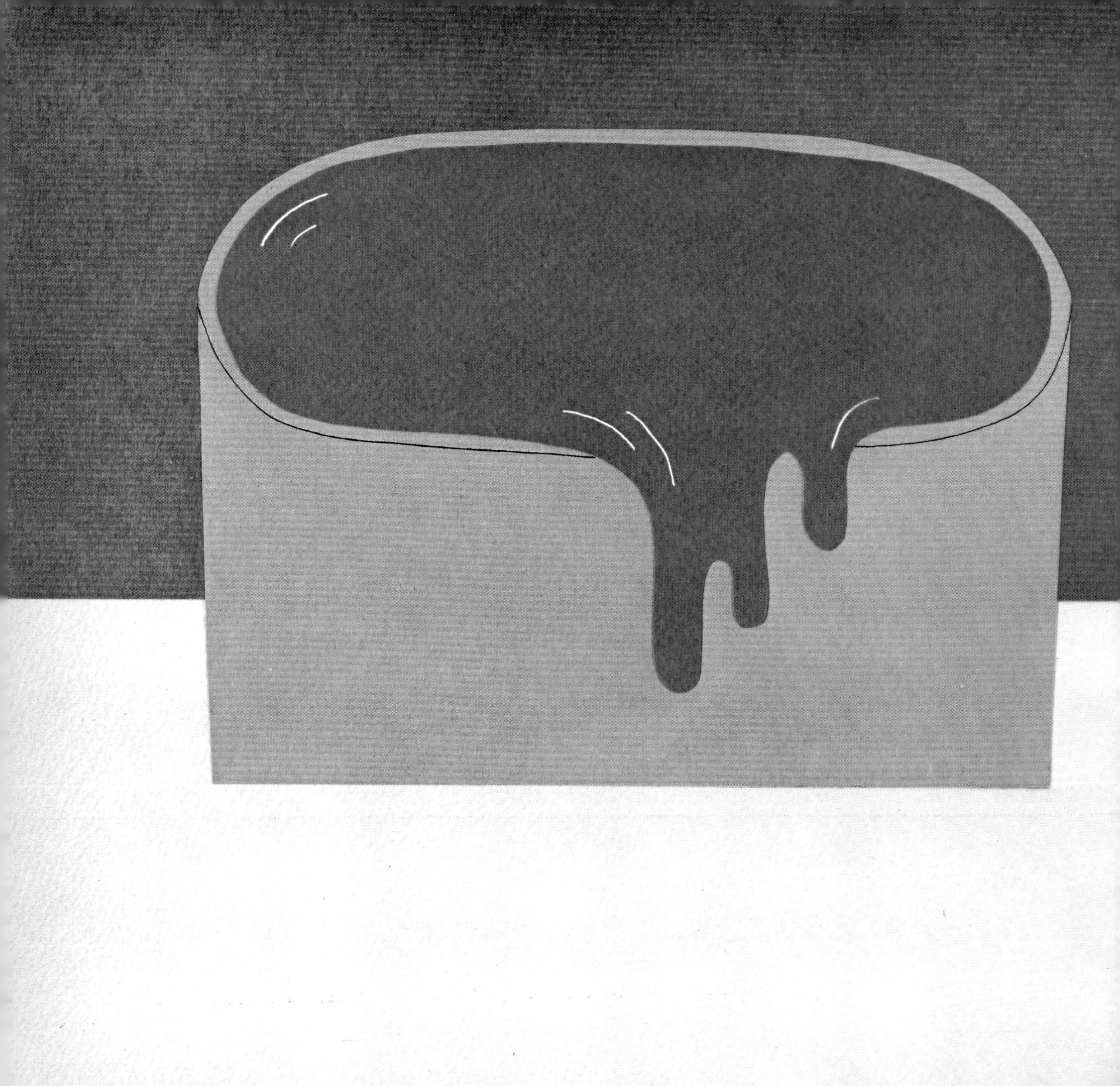

The tub was filled in no time at all. Arthur spoke another magic word to cause the old broom to stop carrying water.

"Cease! Cease! Old broom, cease! You've done your task. . ."

But try as he might, he couldn't remember how to end the spell.

While Arthur was still trying to remember the rest of the magic phrase, the broom continued to carry the water from the river and pour it into the overflowing tub.

The room was flooded, and water streamed out of the door.

"Stop! Stop! I say."

But no matter how loudly he shouted, the old broom continued to carry water.

"Stop it, I say! If you don't stop, I'll. . ."

Arthur picked up an axe and swung it at the broomstick.

The broom split in half, but this did not stop it, for now there were two brooms hauling water.

"Stop it! Stop it! You foolish thing!" Arthur shouted as he swung the axe again and again. But each time he struck a broomstick it split into another one.

The Sorcerer's house was filled with water which all those broomsticks were carrying, until it seemed ready to burst.

"What *shall* I do!" said the frightened Arthur trembling with fear. But just then the Sorcerer arrived home again, and Arthur had to confess what he had done.

"Oh, please forgive me, Master," he pleaded.

The Sorcerer laughed and said, "Now you see what happens when apprentices like you dabble in magic."

Then the Sorcerer called in a loud voice, "Cease! Cease! Old broom, cease! You've done your task. To the corner with you, old broom!"

Instantly the many brooms vanished and only the old broom was left. The water that had filled the house disappeared too.

After that frightening experience, Arthur worked hard, and one day became a famous Sorcerer himself.